VENUS IS A MAN'S WORLD

Start Publishing PD LLC
Copyright © 2024 by Start Publishing PD LLC

Start Publishing PD is a registered trademark of Start Publishing PD LLC
Manufactured in the United States of America

Cover art: Shutterstock/Taisiya Kozorez

Cover design: Jennifer Do

10 9 8 7 6 5 4 3 2 1

ISBN 979-8-8809-2444-8

VENUS IS A MAN'S WORLD

by William Tenn

I've always said that even if Sis is seven years older than me—and a girl besides—she don't always know what's best. Put me on a spaceship jam-packed with three hundred females just aching to get themselves husbands in the one place they're still to be had—the planet Venus—and you know I'll be in trouble.

Bad trouble. With the law, which is the worst a boy can get into.

Twenty minutes after we lifted from the Sahara Spaceport, I wriggled out of my acceleration hammock and started for the door of our cabin.

"Now you be careful, Ferdinand," Sis called after me as she opened a book called *Family Problems of the Frontier Woman*. "Remember you're a nice boy. Don't make me ashamed of you."

I tore down the corridor. Most of the cabins had purple lights on in front of the doors, showing that the girls were still inside their hammocks. That meant only the ship's crew was up and about. Ship's crews are men; women are too busy with important things like government to run ships. I felt free all over—and happy. Now was my chance to really see the *Eleanor Roosevelt*!

*

It was hard to believe I was traveling in space at last. Ahead and behind me, all the way up to where the companionway curved in out of sight, there was nothing but smooth black wall and smooth white doors—on and on and on. *Gee*, I thought excitedly, this is one *big ship*!

Of course, every once in a while I would run across a big scene of stars in the void set in the wall; but they were only pictures. Nothing that gave the feel of great empty space like I'd read about in *The Boy Rocketeers*, no portholes, no visiplates, nothing.

So when I came to the crossway, I stopped for a second, then turned left. To the right, see, there was Deck Four, then Deck Three, leading inward past the engine fo'c'sle to the main jets and the grav helix going *purr-purr-purrty-purr* in the comforting way big machinery has when it's happy and oiled. But to the left, the crossway led all the way to the outside level which ran just under the hull. There were portholes on the hull.

I'd studied all that out in our cabin, long before we'd lifted, on the transparent model of the ship hanging like a big cigar from the ceiling. Sis had studied it too, but she was looking for places like the dining salon and the library and Lifeboat 68 where we should go in case of emergency. I looked for the *important* things.

As I trotted along the crossway, I sort of wished that Sis hadn't decided to go after a husband on a luxury liner. On a cargo ship, now, I'd be climbing from deck to deck on a ladder instead of having gravity underfoot all the time just like I was home on the bottom of the Gulf of Mexico. But women always know what's right, and a boy can only make faces and do what they say, same as the men have to do.

Still, it was pretty exciting to press my nose against the slots in the wall and see the sliding panels that could come charging out and block the crossway into an airtight fit in case a meteor or something smashed into the ship. And all along there were glass cases with spacesuits standing in them, like those knights they used to have back in the Middle Ages.

"In the event of disaster affecting the oxygen content of companionway," they had the words etched into the glass, "break glass with hammer upon wall, remove spacesuit and proceed to don it in the following fashion."

I read the "following fashion" until I knew it by heart. *Boy,* I said to myself, *I hope we have that kind of disaster. I'd sure like to get into one of those! Bet it would be more fun than those diving suits back in Undersea!*

And all the time I was alone. That was the best part.

*

Then I passed Deck Twelve and there was a big sign. "Notice! Passengers not permitted past this point!" A big sign in red.

6

I peeked around the corner. I knew it—the next deck was the hull. I could see the portholes. Every twelve feet, they were, filled with the velvet of space and the dancing of more stars than I'd ever dreamed existed in the Universe.

There wasn't anyone on the deck, as far as I could see. And this distance from the grav helix, the ship seemed mighty quiet and lonely. If I just took one quick look....

But I thought of what Sis would say and I turned around obediently. Then I saw the big red sign again. "Passengers not permitted—"

Well! Didn't I know from my civics class that only women could be Earth Citizens these days? Sure, ever since the Male Desuffrage Act. And didn't I know that you had to be a citizen of a planet in order to get an interplanetary passport? Sis had explained it all to me in the careful, patient way she always talks politics and things like that to men.

"Technically, Ferdinand, I'm the only passenger in our family. You can't be one, because, not being a citizen, you can't acquire an Earth Passport. However, you'll be going to Venus on the strength of this clause—'Miss Evelyn Sparling and all dependent male members of family, this number not to exceed the registered quota of sub-regulations pertaining'—and so on. I want you to understand these matters, so that you will grow into a man who takes an active interest in world affairs. No matter what you hear, women really like and appreciate such men."

Of course, I never pay much attention to Sis when she says such dumb things. I'm old enough, I guess, to know that it isn't what *Women* like and appreciate that counts when it comes to people getting married. If it were, Sis and three hundred other pretty girls like her wouldn't be on their way to Venus to hook husbands.

Still, if I wasn't a passenger, the sign didn't have anything to do with me. I knew what Sis could say to *that*, but at least it was an argument I could use if it ever came up. So I broke the law.

Venus Is a Man's World

I was glad I did. The stars were exciting enough, but away off to the left, about five times as big as I'd ever seen it, except in the movies, was the Moon, a great blob of gray and white pockmarks holding off the black of space. I was hoping to see the Earth, but I figured it must be on the other side of the ship or behind us. I pressed my nose against the port and saw the tiny flicker of a spaceliner taking off, Marsbound. I wished I was on that one!

Then I noticed, a little farther down the companionway, a stretch of blank wall where there should have been portholes. High up on the wall in glowing red letters were the words, "Lifeboat 47. Passengers: Thirty-two. Crew: Eleven. Unauthorized personnel keep away!"

Another one of those signs.

*

I crept up to the porthole nearest it and could just barely make out the stern jets where it was plastered against the hull. Then I walked under the sign and tried to figure the way you were supposed to get into it. There was a very thin line going around in a big circle that I knew must be the door. But I couldn't see any knobs or switches to open it with. Not even a button you could press.

That meant it was a sonic lock like the kind we had on the outer keeps back home in Undersea. But knock or voice? I tried the two knock combinations I knew, and nothing happened. I only remembered one voice key—might as well see if that's it, I figured.

"Twenty, Twenty-three. Open Sesame."

For a second, I thought I'd hit it just right out of all the million possible combinations—The door clicked inward toward a black hole, and a hairy hand as broad as my shoulders shot out of the hole. It closed around my throat and plucked me inside as if I'd been a baby sardine.

I bounced once on the hard lifeboat floor. Before I got my breath and sat up, the door had been shut again. When the light came on,

I found myself staring up the muzzle of a highly polished blaster and into the cold blue eyes of the biggest man I'd ever seen.

He was wearing a one-piece suit made of some scaly green stuff that looked hard and soft at the same time.

His boots were made of it too, and so was the hood hanging down his back.

And his face was brown. Not just ordinary tan, you understand, but the deep, dark, burned-all-the-way-in brown I'd seen on the lifeguards in New Orleans whenever we took a surface vacation—the kind of tan that comes from day after broiling day under a really hot Sun. His hair looked as if it had once been blond, but now there were just long combed-out waves with a yellowish tinge that boiled all the way down to his shoulders.

I hadn't seen hair like that on a man except maybe in history books; every man I'd ever known had his hair cropped in the fashionable soup-bowl style. I was staring at his hair, almost forgetting about the blaster which I knew it was against the law for him to have at all, when I suddenly got scared right through.

His eyes.

They didn't blink and there seemed to be no expression around them. Just coldness. Maybe it was the kind of clothes he was wearing that did it, but all of a sudden I was reminded of a crocodile I'd seen in a surface zoo that had stared quietly at me for twenty minutes until it opened two long tooth-studded jaws.

"Green shatas!" he said suddenly. "Only a tadpole. I must be getting jumpy enough to splash."

Then he shoved the blaster away in a holster made of the same scaly leather, crossed his arms on his chest and began to study me. I grunted to my feet, feeling a lot better. The coldness had gone out of his eyes.

I held out my hand the way Sis had taught me. "My name is Ferdinand Sparling. I'm very pleased to meet you, Mr.—Mr.—"

"Hope for your sake," he said to me, "that you aren't what you seem—tadpole brother to one of them husbandless anura."

"*What?*"

"A 'nuran is a female looking to nest. Anura is a herd of same. Come from Flatfolk ways."

"Flatfolk are the Venusian natives, aren't they? Are you a Venusian? What part of Venus do you come from? Why did you say you hope—"

He chuckled and swung me up into one of the bunks that lined the lifeboat. "Questions you ask," he said in his soft voice. "Venus is a sharp enough place for a dryhorn, let alone a tadpole dryhorn with a boss-minded sister."

"I'm not a dryleg," I told him proudly. "*We're* from Undersea."

"*Dryhorn*, I said, not dryleg. And what's Undersea?"

"Well, in Undersea we called foreigners and newcomers drylegs. Just like on Venus, I guess, you call them dryhorns." And then I told him how Undersea had been built on the bottom of the Gulf of Mexico, when the mineral resources of the land began to give out and engineers figured that a lot could still be reached from the sea bottoms.

*

He nodded. He'd heard about the sea-bottom mining cities that were bubbling under protective domes in every one of the Earth's oceans just about the same time settlements were springing up on the planets.

He looked impressed when I told him about Mom and Pop being one of the first couples to get married in Undersea. He looked thoughtful when I told him how Sis and I had been born there and spent half our childhood listening to the pressure pumps. He raised his eyebrows and looked disgusted when I told how Mom, as Undersea representative on the World Council, had been one of the framers of the Male Desuffrage Act after the Third Atomic War had resulted in the Maternal Revolution.

*

He almost squeezed my arm when I got to the time Mom and Pop were blown up in a surfacing boat.

"Well, after the funeral, there was a little money, so Sis decided we might as well use it to migrate. There was no future for her on Earth, she figured. You know, the three-out-of-four."

"How's that?"

"The three-out-of-four. No more than three women out of every four on Earth can expect to find husbands. Not enough men to go around. Way back in the Twentieth Century, it began to be felt, Sis says, what with the wars and all. Then the wars went on and a lot more men began to die or get no good from the radioactivity. Then the best men went to the planets, Sis says, until by now even if a woman can scrounge a personal husband, he's not much to boast about."

The stranger nodded violently. "Not on Earth, he isn't. Those busybody anura make sure of that. What a place! Suffering gridniks, I had a bellyful!"

He told me about it. Women were scarce on Venus, and he hadn't been able to find any who were willing to come out to his lonely little islands; he had decided to go to Earth where there was supposed to be a surplus. Naturally, having been born and brought up on a very primitive planet, he didn't know "it's a woman's world," like the older boys in school used to say.

The moment he landed on Earth he was in trouble. He didn't know he had to register at a government-operated hotel for transient males; he threw a bartender through a thick plastic window for saying something nasty about the length of his hair; and *imagine!*—he not only resisted arrest, resulting in three hospitalized policemen, but he sassed the judge in open court!

"Told me a man wasn't supposed to say anything except through female attorneys. Told *her* that where *I* came from, a man spoke his piece when he'd a mind to, and his woman walked by his side."

11

Venus Is a Man's World

"What happened?" I asked breathlessly.

"Oh, Guilty of This and Contempt of That. That blown-up brinosaur took my last munit for fines, then explained that she was remitting the rest because I was a foreigner and uneducated." His eyes grew dark for a moment. He chuckled again. "But I wasn't going to serve all those fancy little prison sentences. Forcible Citizenship Indoctrination, they call it? Shook the dead-dry dust of the misbegotten, God forsaken mother world from my feet forever. The women on it deserve their men. My pockets were folded from the fines, and the paddlefeet were looking for me so close I didn't dare radio for more munit. So I stowed away."

*

For a moment, I didn't understand him. When I did, I was almost ill. "Y-you mean," I choked, "th-that you're b-breaking the law right now? And I'm with you while you're doing it?"

He leaned over the edge of the bunk and stared at me very seriously. "What breed of tadpole are they turning out these days? Besides, what business do *you* have this close to the hull?"

After a moment of sober reflection, I nodded. "You're right. I've also become a male outside the law. We're in this together."

He guffawed. Then he sat up and began cleaning his blaster. I found myself drawn to the bright killer-tube with exactly the fascination Sis insists such things have always had for men.

"Ferdinand your label? That's not right for a sprouting tadpole. I'll call you Ford. My name's Butt. Butt Lee Brown."

I liked the sound of Ford. "Is Butt a nickname, too?"

"Yeah. Short for Alberta, but I haven't found a man who can draw a blaster fast enough to call me that. You see, Pop came over in the eighties—the big wave of immigrants when they evacuated Ontario. Named all us boys after Canadian provinces. I was the youngest, so I got the name they were saving for a girl."

"You had a lot of brothers, Mr. Butt?"

He grinned with a mighty set of teeth. "Oh, a nestful. Of course, they were all killed in the Blue Chicago Rising by the MacGregor boys—all except me and Saskatchewan. Then Sas and me hunted the MacGregors down. Took a heap of time; we didn't float Jock MacGregor's ugly face down the Tuscany till both of us were pretty near grown up."

I walked up close to where I could see the tiny bright copper coils of the blaster above the firing button. "Have you killed a lot of men with that, Mr. Butt?"

"Butt. Just plain Butt to you, Ford." He frowned and sighted at the light globe. "No more'n twelve—not counting five government paddlefeet, of course. I'm a peaceable planter. Way I figure it, violence never accomplishes much that's important. My brother Sas, now—"

*

He had just begun to work into a wonderful anecdote about his brother when the dinner gong rang. Butt told me to scat. He said I was a growing tadpole and needed my vitamins. And he mentioned, very off-hand, that he wouldn't at all object if I brought him some fresh fruit. It seemed there was nothing but processed foods in the lifeboat and Butt was used to a farmer's diet.

Trouble was, he was a special kind of farmer. Ordinary fruit would have been pretty easy to sneak into my pockets at meals. I even found a way to handle the kelp and giant watercress Mr. Brown liked, but things like seaweed salt and Venusian mud-grapes just had too strong a smell. Twice, the mechanical hamper refused to accept my jacket for laundering and I had to wash it myself. But I learned so many wonderful things about Venus every time I visited that stowaway....

I learned three wild-wave songs of the Flatfolk and what it is that the native Venusians hate so much; I learned how you tell the difference between a lousy government paddlefoot from New Kalamazoo and the slaptoe slinker who is the planter's friend. After a lot of begging, Butt Lee Brown explained the workings of his blaster, explained it so carefully that I could name every part and tell what it did from the tiny round electrodes to the long spirals of transformer. But no matter what, he would never let me hold it.

"Sorry, Ford, old tad," he would drawl, spinning around and around in the control swivel-chair at the nose of the lifeboat. "But way I look at it, a man who lets somebody else handle his blaster is like the giant whose heart was in an egg that an enemy found. When you've grown enough so's your pop feels you ought to have a weapon, why, then's the time to learn it and you might's well learn fast. Before then, you're plain too young to be even near it."

"I don't have a father to give me one when I come of age. I don't even have an older brother as head of my family like your brother Labrador. All I have is Sis. And *she*—"

"She'll marry some fancy dryhorn who's never been farther South than the Polar Coast. And she'll stay head of the family, if I know her breed of green shata. *Bossy, opinionated.* By the way, Fordie," he said, rising and stretching so the fish-leather bounced and rippled off his biceps, "that sister. She ever...."

And he'd be off again, cross-examining me about Evelyn. I sat in the swivel chair he'd vacated and tried to answer his questions. But there was a lot of stuff I didn't know. Evelyn was a healthy girl, for instance; how healthy, exactly, I had no way of finding out. Yes, I'd tell him, my aunts on both sides of my family each had had more than the average number of children. No, we'd never done any farming to speak of, back in Undersea, but—yes, I'd guess Evelyn knew about as much as any girl there when it came to diving equipment and pressure pump regulation.

How would I know that stuff would lead to trouble for me?

*

Sis had insisted I come along to the geography lecture. Most of the other girls who were going to Venus for husbands talked to each other during the lecture, but not *my* sister! She hung on every word,

14

took notes even, and asked enough questions to make the perspiring purser really work in those orientation periods.

"I am very sorry, Miss Sparling," he said with pretty heavy sarcasm, "but I cannot remember any of the agricultural products of the Macro Continent. Since the human population is well below one per thousand square miles, it can readily be understood that the quantity of tilled soil, land or sub-surface, is so small that—Wait, I remember something. The Macro Continent exports a fruit though not exactly an edible one. The wild *dunging* drug is harvested there by criminal speculators. Contrary to belief on Earth, the traffic has been growing in recent years. In fact—"

"Pardon me, sir," I broke in, "but doesn't *dunging* come only from Leif Erickson Island off the Moscow Peninsula of the Macro Continent? You remember, purser—Wang Li's third exploration, where he proved the island and the peninsula didn't meet for most of the year?"

The purser nodded slowly. "I forgot," he admitted. "Sorry, ladies, but the boy's right. Please make the correction in your notes."

But Sis was the only one who took notes, and she didn't take that one. She stared at me for a moment, biting her lower lip thoughtfully, while I got sicker and sicker. Then she shut her pad with the final gesture of the right hand that Mom used to use just before challenging the opposition to come right down on the Council floor and debate it out with her.

"Ferdinand," Sis said, "let's go back to our cabin."

The moment she sat me down and walked slowly around me, I knew I was in for it. "I've been reading up on Venusian geography in the ship's library," I told her in a hurry.

"No doubt," she said drily. She shook her night-black hair out. "But you aren't going to tell me that you read about *dunging* in the ship's library. The books there have been censored by a government agent of Earth against the possibility that they might be read by susceptible young male minds like yours. She would not have allowed—this Terran Agent—"

"Paddlefoot," I sneered.

Sis sat down hard in our zoom-air chair. "Now that's a term," she said carefully, "that is used only by Venusian riffraff."

"They're not!"

"Not what?"

"Riffraff," I had to answer, knowing I was getting in deeper all the time and not being able to help it. I mustn't give Mr. Brown away! "They're trappers and farmers, pioneers and explorers, who're building Venus. And it takes a real man to build on a hot, hungry hell like Venus."

"Does it, now?" she said, looking at me as if I were beginning to grow a second pair of ears. "Tell me more."

"You can't have meek, law-abiding, women-ruled men when you start civilization on a new planet. You've got to have men who aren't afraid to make their own law if necessary—with their own guns. That's where law begins; the books get written up later."

"You're going to *tell*, Ferdinand, what evil, criminal male is speaking through your mouth!"

"Nobody!" I insisted. "They're my own ideas!"

"They are remarkably well-organized for a young boy's ideas. A boy who, I might add, has previously shown a ridiculous but nonetheless entirely masculine boredom with political philosophy. I plan to have a government career on that new planet you talk about, Ferdinand—after I have found a good, steady husband, of course—and I don't look forward to a masculinist radical in the family. Now, who has been filling your head with all this nonsense?"

*

I was sweating. Sis has that deadly bulldog approach when she feels someone is lying. I pulled my pulpast handkerchief from my pocket to wipe my face. Something rattled to the floor.

"What is this picture of me doing in your pocket, Ferdinand?"

A trap seemed to be hinging noisily into place. "One of the passengers wanted to see how you looked in a bathing suit."

"The passengers on this ship are all female. I can't imagine any of them that curious about my appearance. Ferdinand, it's a man who has been giving you these anti-social ideas, isn't it? A war-mongering masculinist like all the frustrated men who want to engage in government and don't have the vaguest idea how to. Except, of course, in their ancient, bloody ways. Ferdinand, who has been perverting that sunny and carefree soul of yours?"

"Nobody! *Nobody!*"

"Ferdinand, there's no point in lying! I demand—"

"I told you, Sis. I told you! And don't call me Ferdinand. Call me Ford."

"Ford? *Ford?* Now, you listen to me, Ferdinand...."

After that it was all over but the confession. That came in a few moments. I couldn't fool Sis. She just knew me too well, I decided miserably. Besides, she was a girl.

All the same, I wouldn't get Mr. Butt Lee Brown into trouble if I could help it. I made Sis promise she wouldn't turn him in if I took her to him. And the quick, nodding way she said she would made me feel just a little better.

The door opened on the signal, "Sesame." When Butt saw somebody was with me, he jumped and the ten-inch blaster barrel grew out of his fingers. Then he recognized Sis from the pictures.

He stepped to one side and, with the same sweeping gesture, holstered his blaster and pushed his green hood off. It was Sis's turn to jump when she saw the wild mass of hair rolling down his back.

"An honor, Miss Sparling," he said in that rumbly voice. "Please come right in. There's a hurry-up draft."

So Sis went in and I followed right after her. Mr. Brown closed the door. I tried to catch his eye so I could give him some kind of hint or explanation, but he had taken a couple of his big strides and was in the control section with Sis. She didn't give ground, though; I'll say

17

that for her. She only came to his chest, but she had her arms crossed sternly.

"First, Mr. Brown," she began, like talking to a cluck of a kid in class, "you realize that you are not only committing the political crime of traveling without a visa, and the criminal one of stowing away without paying your fare, but the moral delinquency of consuming stores intended for the personnel of this ship solely in emergency?"

*

He opened his mouth to its maximum width and raised an enormous hand. Then he let the air out and dropped his arm.

"I take it you either have no defense or care to make none," Sis added caustically.

Butt laughed slowly and carefully as if he were going over each word. "Wonder if all the anura talk like that. And *you* want to foul up Venus."

"We haven't done so badly on Earth, after the mess you men made of politics. It needed a revolution of the mothers before—"

"Needed nothing. Everyone wanted peace. Earth is a weary old world."

"It's a world of strong moral fiber compared to yours, Mr. Alberta Lee Brown." Hearing his rightful name made him move suddenly and tower over her. Sis said with a certain amount of hurry and change of tone, "What *do* you have to say about stowing away and using up lifeboat stores?"

*

He cocked his head and considered a moment. "Look," he said finally, "I have more than enough munit to pay for round trip tickets, but I couldn't get a return visa because of that brinosaur judge and all the charges she hung on me. Had to stow away. Picked the *Eleanor Roosevelt* because a couple of the boys in the crew are friends of mine and they were willing to help. But this lifeboat—don't you know that every passenger ship carries four times as many lifeboats as it needs? Not to mention the food I didn't eat because it stuck in my throat?"

"Yes," she said bitterly. "You had this boy steal fresh fruit for you. I suppose you didn't know that under space regulations that makes him equally guilty?"

"No, Sis, he didn't," I was beginning to argue. "All he wanted—"

"Sure I knew. Also know that if I'm picked up as a stowaway, I'll be sent back to Earth to serve out those fancy little sentences."

"Well, you're guilty of them, aren't you?"

He waved his hands at her impatiently. "I'm not talking law, female; I'm talking sense. Listen! I'm in trouble because I went to Earth to look for a wife. You're standing here right now because you're on your way to Venus for a husband. So let's."

Sis actually staggered back. "Let's? Let's *what*? Are—are you daring to suggest that—that—"

"Now, Miss Sparling, no hoopla. I'm saying let's get married, and you know it. You figured out from what the boy told you that I was chewing on you for a wife. You're healthy and strong, got good heredity, you know how to operate sub-surface machinery, you've lived underwater, and your disposition's no worse than most of the anura I've seen. Prolific stock, too."

I was so excited I just had to yell: "Gee, Sis, say *yes*!"

*

My sister's voice was steaming with scorn. "And what makes you think that I'd consider you a desirable husband?"

He spread his hands genially. "Figure if you wanted a poodle, you're pretty enough to pick one up on Earth. Figure if you charge off to Venus, you don't want a poodle, you want a man. I'm one. I own three islands in the Galertan Archipelago that'll be good oozing mudgrape land when they're cleared. Not to mention the rich berzeliot beds offshore. I got no bad habits outside of having my own way. I'm also passable good-looking for a slaptoe planter. Besides, if you marry me you'll be the first mated on this ship—and that's a splash most nesting females like to make."

There was a longish stretch of quiet. Sis stepped back and measured him slowly with her eyes; there was a lot to look at. He waited patiently while she covered the distance from his peculiar green boots to that head of hair. I was so excited I was gulping instead of breathing. Imagine having Butt for a brother-in-law and living on a wet-plantation in Flatfolk country!

But then I remembered Sis's level head and I didn't have much hope any more.

"You know," she began, "there's more to marriage than just—"

"So there is," he cut in. "Well, we can try each other for taste." And he pulled her in, both of his great hands practically covering her slim, straight back.

Neither of them said anything for a bit after he let go. Butt spoke up first.

"Now, me," he said, "I'd vote yes."

Sis ran the tip of her tongue kind of delicately from side to side of her mouth. Then she stepped back slowly and looked at him as if she were figuring out how many feet high he was. She kept on moving backward, tapping her chin, while Butt and I got more and more impatient. When she touched the lifeboat door, she pushed it open and jumped out.

*

Butt ran over and looked down the crossway. After a while, he shut the door and came back beside me. "Well," he said, swinging to a bunk, "that's sort of it."

"You're better off, Butt," I burst out. "You shouldn't have a woman like Sis for a wife. She looks small and helpless, but don't forget she was trained to run an underwater city!"

"Wasn't worrying about that," he grinned. "I grew up in the fifteen long years of the Blue Chicago Rising. Nope." He turned over on his back and clicked his teeth at the ceiling. "Think we'd have nested out nicely."

I hitched myself up to him and we sat on the bunk, glooming away at each other. Then we heard the tramp of feet in the crossway.

Butt swung down and headed for the control compartment in the nose of the lifeboat. He had his blaster out and was cursing very interestingly. I started after him, but he picked me up by the seat of my jumper and tossed me toward the door. The Captain came in and tripped over me.

I got all tangled up in his gold braid and million-mile space buttons. When we finally got to our feet and sorted out right, he was breathing very hard. The Captain was a round little man with a plump, golden face and a very scared look on it. He *humphed* at me, just the way Sis does, and lifted me by the scruff of my neck. The Chief Mate picked me up and passed me to the Second Assistant Engineer.

Sis was there, being held by the purser on one side and the Chief Computer's Mate on the other. Behind them, I could see a flock of wide-eyed female passengers.

"You cowards!" Sis was raging. "Letting your Captain face a dangerous outlaw all by himself!"

"I dunno, Miss Sparling," the Computer's Mate said, scratching the miniature slide-rule insignia on his visor with his free hand. "The Old Man would've been willing to let it go with a log entry, figuring the spaceport paddlefeet could pry out the stowaway when we landed. But you had to quote the Mother Anita Law at him, and he's in there doing his duty. He figures the rest of us are family men, too, and there's no sense making orphans."

"You promised, Sis," I told her through my teeth. "You promised you wouldn't get Butt into trouble!"

She tossed her spiral curls at me and ground a heel into the purser's instep. He screwed up his face and howled, but he didn't let go of her arm.

"*Shush*, Ferdinand, this is serious!"

It was. I heard the Captain say, "I'm not carrying a weapon, Brown."

"Then *get* one," Butt's low, lazy voice floated out.

"No, thanks. You're as handy with that thing as I am with a rocketboard." The Captain's words got a little fainter as he walked forward. Butt growled like a gusher about to blow.

"I'm counting on your being a good guy, Brown." The Captain's voice quavered just a bit. "I'm banking on what I heard about the blast-happy Browns every time I lifted gravs in New Kalamazoo; they have a code, they don't burn unarmed men."

*

Just about this time, events in the lifeboat went down to a mumble. The top of my head got wet and I looked up. There was sweat rolling down the Second Assistant's forehead; it converged at his nose and bounced off the tip in a sizable stream. I twisted out of the way.

"What's happening?" Sis gritted, straining toward the lock.

"Butt's trying to decide whether he wants him fried or scrambled," the Computer's Mate said, pulling her back. "Hey, purse, remember when the whole family with their pop at the head went into Heatwave to argue with Colonel Leclerc?"

"Eleven dead, sixty-four injured," the purser answered mechanically. "And no more army stationed south of Icebox." His right ear twitched irritably. "But what're they saying?"

Suddenly we heard. "By authority vested in me under the Pomona College Treaty," the Captain was saying very loudly, "I arrest you for violation of Articles Sixteen to Twenty-one inclusive of the Space Transport Code, and order your person and belongings impounded for the duration of this voyage as set forth in Sections Forty-one and Forty-five—"

"Forty-three and Forty-five," Sis groaned. "Sections Forty-three and Forty-five, I told him. I even made him repeat it after me!"

WILLIAM TENN

"—of the Mother Anita Law, SC 2136, Emergency Interplanetary Directives."

*

We all waited breathlessly for Butt's reply. The seconds ambled on and there was no clatter of electrostatic discharge, no smell of burning flesh.

Then we heard some feet walking. A big man in a green suit swung out into the crossway. That was Butt. Behind him came the Captain, holding the blaster gingerly with both hands. Butt had a funny, thoughtful look on his face.

The girls surged forward when they saw him, scattering the crew to one side. They were like a school of sharks that had just caught sight of a dying whale.

"M-m-m-m! Are all Venusians built like that?"

"Men like that are worth the mileage!"

"*I want him!*" "*I want him!*" "*I want him!*"

Sis had been let go. She grabbed my free hand and pulled me away. She was trying to look only annoyed, but her eyes had bright little bubbles of fury popping in them.

"The cheap extroverts! And they call themselves responsible women!"

I was angry, too. And I let her know, once we were in our cabin. "What about that promise, Sis? You said you wouldn't turn him in. You *promised*!"

She stopped walking around the room as if she had been expecting to get to Venus on foot. "I know I did, Ferdinand, but he forced me."

"My name is Ford and I don't understand."

"Your name is Ferdinand and stop trying to act forcefully like a girl. It doesn't become you. In just a few days, you'll forget all this and be your simple, carefree self again. I really truly meant to keep my word. From what you'd told me, Mr. Brown seemed to be a fundamentally decent chap despite his barbaric notions on equality between the sexes—or worse. I was positive I could shame him into a more

23

rational social behavior and make him give himself up. Then he—he—"

She pressed her fingernails into her palms and let out a long, glaring sigh at the door. "Then he kissed me! Oh, it was a good enough kiss—Mr. Brown has evidently had a varied and colorful background—but the galling idiocy of the man, trying that! I was just getting over the colossal impudence involved in *his* proposing marriage—as if *he* had to bear the children!—and was considering the offer seriously, on its merits, as one should consider *all* suggestions, when he deliberately dropped the pretense of reason. He appealed to me as most of the savage ancients appealed to their women, as an emotional machine. Throw the correct sexual switches, says this theory, and the female surrenders herself ecstatically to the doubtful and bloody murk of masculine plans."

*

There was a double knock on the door and the Captain walked in without waiting for an invitation. He was still holding Butt's blaster. He pointed it at me. "Get your hands up, Ferdinand Sparling," he said.

I did.

"I hereby order your detention for the duration of this voyage, for aiding and abetting a stowaway, as set forth in Sections Forty-one and Forty-five—"

"Forty-three and Forty-five," Sis interrupted him, her eyes getting larger and rounder. "But you gave me your word of honor that no charges would be lodged against the boy!"

"Forty-one and Forty-five," he corrected her courteously, still staring fiercely at me. "I looked it up. Of the Anita Mason Law, Emergency Interplanetary Directives. That was the usual promise one makes to an informer, but I made it before I knew it was Butt Lee Brown you were talking about. I didn't want to arrest Butt Lee Brown. You forced me. So I'm breaking my promise to you, just as, I understand, you broke your promise to your brother. They'll both

24

be picked up at New Kalamazoo Spaceport and sent Terraward for trial."

"But I used all of our money to buy passage," Sis wailed.

"And now you'll have to return with the boy. I'm sorry, Miss Sparling. But as you explained to me, a man who has been honored with an important official position should stay close to the letter of the law for the sake of other men who are trying to break down terrestrial anti-male prejudice. Of course, there's a way out."

"There is? Tell me, please!"

"Can I lower my hands a minute?" I asked.

"No, you can't, son—not according to the armed surveillance provisions of the Mother Anita Law. Miss Sparling, if you'd marry Brown—now, now, don't look at me like that!—we could let the whole matter drop. A shipboard wedding and he goes on your passport as a 'dependent male member of family,' which means, so far as the law is concerned, that he had a regulation passport from the beginning of this voyage. And once we touch Venusian soil he can contact his bank and pay for passage. On the record, no crime was ever committed. He's free, the boy's free, and you—"

"—Are married to an uncombed desperado who doesn't know enough to sit back and let a woman run things. Oh, you should be ashamed!"

*

The Captain shrugged and spread his arms wide.

"Perhaps I should be, but that's what comes of putting men into responsible positions, as you would say. See here, Miss Sparling, I didn't want to arrest Brown, and, if it's at all possible, I'd still prefer not to. The crew, officers and men, all go along with me. We may be legal residents of Earth, but our work requires us to be on Venus several times a year. We don't want to be disliked by any members of the highly irritable Brown clan or its collateral branches. Butt Lee Brown himself, for all of his savage appearance in your civilized eyes, is a man of much influence on the Polar Continent. In his own bailiwick, the Galertan Archipelago, he makes, breaks and occasionally readjusts officials. Then there's his brother Saskatchewan who considers Butt a helpless, put-upon youngster—"

"Much influence, you say? Mr. Brown has?" Sis was suddenly thoughtful.

"*Power*, actually. The kind a strong man usually wields in a newly settled community. Besides, Miss Sparling, you're going to Venus for a husband because the male-female ratio on Earth is reversed. Well, not only is Butt Lee Brown a first class catch, but you can't afford to be too particular in any case. While you're fairly pretty, you won't bring any wealth into a marriage and your high degree of opinionation is not likely to be well-received on a backward, masculinist world. Then, too, the woman-hunger is not so great any more, what with the *Marie Curie* and the *Fatima* having already deposited their cargoes, the *Mme. Sun Yat Sen* due to arrive next month...."

*

Sis nodded to herself, waved the door open, and walked out.

"Let's hope," the Captain said. "Like any father used to say, a man who knows how to handle women, how to get around them without their knowing it, doesn't need to know anything else in this life. I'm plain wasted in space. You can lower your hands now, son."

We sat down and I explained the blaster to him. He was very interested. He said all Butt had told him—in the lifeboat when they decided to use my arrest as a club over Sis—was to keep the safety catch all the way up against his thumb. I could see he really had been excited about carrying a lethal weapon around. He told me that back in the old days, captains—sea captains, that is—actually had the right to keep guns in their cabins all the time to put down mutinies and other things our ancestors did.

The telewall flickered, and we turned it on. Sis smiled down. "Everything's all right, Captain. Come up and marry us, please."

"What did you stick him for?" he asked. "What was the price?"

Sis's full lips went thin and hard, the way Mom's used to. Then she thought better of it and laughed. "Mr. Brown is going to see that I'm elected sheriff of the Galertan Archipelago."

"And I thought she'd settle for a county clerkship!" the Captain muttered as we spun up to the brig.

The doors were open and girls were chattering in every corner. Sis came up to the Captain to discuss arrangements. I slipped away and found Butt sitting with folded arms in a corner of the brig. He grinned at me. "Hi, tadpole. Like the splash?"

I shook my head unhappily. "Butt, why did you do it? I'd sure love to be your brother-in-law, but, gosh, you didn't have to marry Sis." I pointed at some of the bustling females. Sis was going to have three hundred bridesmaids. "Any one of them would have jumped at the chance to be your wife. And once on any woman's passport, you'd be free. Why Sis?"

"That's what the Captain said in the lifeboat. Told him same thing I'm telling you. I'm stubborn. What I like at first, I keep on liking. What I want at first, I keep on wanting until I get."

"Yes, but making Sis sheriff! And you'll have to back her up with your blaster. What'll happen to that man's world?"

"Wait'll after we nest and go out to my islands." He produced a hard-lipped, smug grin, sighting it at Sis's slender back. "She'll find herself sheriff over a bunch of natives and exactly two Earth males—you and me. I got a hunch that'll keep her pretty busy, though."

www.ingramcontent.com/pod-product-compliance
Lightning Source LLC
Chambersburg PA
CBHW020349130626
46549CB00003B/1379